THE Magic PORRIDGE POT

Margaret McAllister

Illustrated by
Peter Utton

OXFORD
UNIVERSITY PRESS

Great Clarendon Street, Oxford OX2 6DP

Oxford University Press is a department of the University of Oxford.
It furthers the University's objective of excellence in research, scholarship,
and education by publishing worldwide in

Oxford   New York

Auckland   Cape Town   Dar es Salaam   Hong Kong   Karachi
Kuala Lumpur   Madrid   Melbourne   Mexico City   Nairobi
New Delhi   Shanghai   Taipei   Toronto

With offices in

Argentina   Austria   Brazil   Chile   Czech Republic   France   Greece
Guatemala   Hungary   Italy   Japan   Poland   Portugal   Singapore
South Korea   Switzerland   Thailand   Turkey   Ukraine   Vietnam

Oxford is a registered trade mark of Oxford University Press
in the UK and in certain other countries

British Library Cataloguing in Publication Data

Data available

ISBN 978-0-19-915161-5

1 3 5 7 9 10 8 6 4 2

Mixed Pack (1 of 6 different titles): ISBN 978-0-19-915160-8
Class Pack (6 copies of 6 titles): ISBN 978-0-19-915159-2

Printed in China by Imago

Contents

Chapter 1

The House of Children

At the end of the village was Mrs Molly's house. It had a big garden and it was always full of children.

None of them were Mrs Molly's own children. They had nobody else to look after them, so Mrs Molly did.

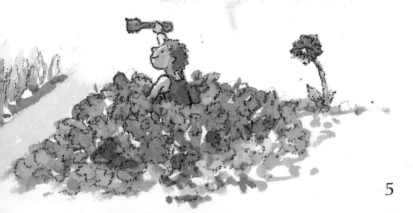

They were:

Charlie, who was
still a baby,

Pippa, who was
nearly grown-up,

and Paul and
Jenny, who
were in-between.

Mrs Molly worried about Paul. He was
small for his age, and never spoke.

Mrs Molly and the children grew
carrots and cabbages, parsnips and
potatoes, sprouts and spinach, and lots
and lots and lots of lettuce. Mrs Molly
needed the vegetables to feed them all.

"The children must never go hungry,"
said Mrs Molly. But sometimes it was
hard to feed everyone.

One winter day, when the frost was as
white as sugar and as hard as stone,
Pippa went to the village.

When she came home, she was so cold
that her face was pale and her nose was
pink. Beside her was a very old woman
carrying a bundle.

"I met her on the way home," said Pippa to Mrs Molly. "She is on a long journey. She has nowhere to sleep tonight, so I brought her home."

"Good," said Mrs Molly. "Bring her in to get warm."

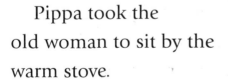

Pippa took the old woman to sit by the warm stove.

There was only soup for supper that night, but Mrs Molly made sure that everyone had a share.

In the morning, when Mrs Molly and the children got up, the old woman had gone. On the stove stood a large stone bowl with a lid on, and a note.

This is the magic porridge pot. It will never leave a child disappointed.

Chapter *2*

Magic for Breakfast

The children stood round the porridge pot. Pippa held on to Charlie in case it was hot. Mrs Molly lifted the lid.

"Ooh!" said Charlie.

"I'm hungry!" said Jenny.

Paul said nothing, but his eyes looked very big.

The pot was full of steamy, creamy, hot, sweet porridge. It tasted of cream and honey. It made them feel warm inside. Everybody had second helpings.

Every morning in winter the pot was full of steamy, creamy porridge. That is, every morning except Jenny's birthday.

That day, they found a cake with six candles in the porridge pot instead.

After the icy winter
came the spring. Daffodils grew in
the garden. The children woke up one
morning and sniffed. A very nice smell
was coming from the porridge pot.

"It smells warm," said Jenny.

"It smells like something that isn't
porridge," said Pippa.

"Ooh!" said Charlie.

Paul said nothing at all.

"It smells like fresh bread," said Mrs Molly. She took off the lid.

The smell was so delicious that everyone felt empty inside.
Pippa lifted Charlie up.
Paul stood on tiptoe.

The pot was full of fresh, hot bread.
There was crusty bread, soft bread, brown
bread and shiny white bread. There were
curly rolls and twisty rolls. There were
rolls with sesame seeds on top.

"Breakfast time," said Mrs Molly.

All through the spring, the porridge pot made bread.

It made crumpets, muffins, and teacakes.

On Sundays, it made sticky buns.

Chapter 3

Summer Magic

The days grew longer and longer
and warmer and warmer.

One morning, when the sun rose and
woke the birds, and the birds sang and
woke the children, they all went with Mrs
Molly to look in the porridge pot.

"It's very cold," said Mrs Molly, as she
took off the lid.

"It's pink and creamy," said Jenny.
"It's yoghurt," said Pippa.
"Og!" said Charlie.
Paul said nothing at all.

"Strawberry yoghurt!" said Mrs Molly.
"Bring your bowls!"

All summer, the porridge pot gave
them thick, swirly-whirly yoghurt.
It might be strawberry, raspberry, banana,
or pineapple, toffee, or lemon.

There was a chocolate cake on Pippa's
birthday.

There was a birthday cake for Charlie
with sweets on top, and two blue
candles.

The days grew shorter and cooler.

Birds gathered on the rooftops, ready to fly away. The leaves on the trees turned yellow.

One cold morning in October, Mrs Molly took the lid off the porridge pot.

Yum!

Paul said nothing, but his eyes looked enormous.

"Apple pie for breakfast!" said Mrs Molly.

The next day, it was chicken pie. The day after that, there was blackberry pie. Then vegetable pie.

The porridge pot made a different pie every day for two weeks.

Then it started again with apple pie. For Mrs Molly's birthday, it made a cherry cake with nuts on the top instead of candles.

"It will be Paul's birthday next," said Mrs Molly.

Paul nodded, but he said nothing.

Chapter 4

The Best Magic

Winter came again. There was frost on
the windows and ice on the path.

One night, as the children were going
to bed, the snow began to fall.

"I think the porridge pot will
do something new tomorrow," said
Mrs Molly. "I wonder what it will be?"

Paul said nothing. But when they were all tucked up in bed, he could not sleep.

Long ago, when Paul was little, before he came to live with Mrs Molly, he was always hungry. There was never enough to eat.

He could remember a day when he was very small and hungry. He had stood in the street and looked at a market stall full of fruit.

There were bananas like big yellow smiles …

… and oranges like sunshine.

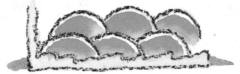

There were raspberries, strawberries and cherries as bright as jewels.

The woman at the stall had smiled kindly. She had given him a cherry. It tasted as sweet as summer.

Ever since then, Paul had dreamed of cherries. He hoped and wished for cherries from the porridge pot.

He got up and crept down to the kitchen. The porridge pot stood on the stove. He tiptoed over the cold floor in his bare feet. He stretched up to hug the porridge pot.

"Please," he whispered, "Cherries. Cherries, please."

Paul was very small and the pot was very big. On tiptoe on the cold floor, he wobbled. He lost his balance.

He fell, and the porridge pot tipped. It tumbled. And it smashed and crashed on to the floor!

Paul shut his eyes. He opened his mouth and screamed out a long, loud cry.

Curled up on the floor with the broken pieces of the pot, he cried and cried.

Everyone woke up.

Everyone ran downstairs. Mrs Molly put Paul on her knee and hugged him. He wanted to say he was very sorry, but he was crying too much.

"Paul!" said Mrs Molly. "Look what happened!"

Paul said nothing. He hurt with crying.

"Paul," said Mrs Molly kindly. "Look!"

Paul dried his eyes. He looked.

Nobody was cross with him.

Everybody smiled.

On the floor there were FOUR porridge pots.

One was full of hot buttery potatoes in their jackets.

One would not open at all. It had a label on it that said: *For Christmas Day and Paul's birthday*. It smelt lovely.

One was full of big yellow bananas and sunny oranges.

Mrs Molly took the lid off the last one.

It was full of bright red strawberries, pink raspberries, and ...

"CHERRIES!" shouted Paul.

"Dark, plump, shiny cherries!" said Mrs Molly.

"Yummy," said Jenny.

"They look like jewels," said Pippa.

"Ooh!" said Charlie.

"Thank you," said Paul.

About the author

I first thought of this story long ago, and told it to my children when they were younger. I wish I had a magic porridge pot, to feed all the hungry people in the world.

I have met lots of kind, warm people like Mrs Molly. They feed anyone who's hungry, and are never too busy – a bit like the porridge pot!